SPREADING
CHRISTMAS JOY

TORY BAKER

SPREADING
CHRISTMAS
Joy

TORY BAKER

Spreading Christmas Joy
Tory Baker
torybakerbooks@gmail.com

Copyright © 2017 by Tory Baker

Cover Designer: Romantic Book Affairs

Joy loves everything about Christmas.

Her town has even nicknamed Christmas Joy.

Eb is a recluse who has no time for the holiday.

When Joy comes over to share her cookies and spreading Christmas cheer, there's only one thing that Eb wants to spread.

Joy.

This standalone Christmas novella is hot enough to put you on Santa's naughty list and give you visions of a lot more than sugar plums dancing.

1

Joy

"Joy! Your delivery is here!" Tina calls from the front of the shop. I barely stop myself from clapping. I've been waiting for that delivery all day!

"Be right there!" I call, sending up a silent prayer of thanks for Amazon's quick delivery service. I wipe my hands on my apron, looking at the wedding cake I just frosted. It's a clean white everywhere with a sprinkling of silver glitter dust to give the effect of new snowfall. Naomi is going to love her cake and I'm going to love the business her wedding brings my business.

I run Comfort and Joy bakery. I've built it from scratch, so to speak, and slowly it's taken off. This Christmas will mark my second year in business and I've loved every moment of it. There have been months I wasn't sure I was going to make the rent, but somehow, through it all, I've survived. This wedding is my biggest account yet. Naomi is a local celebrity—she anchors the local news—and her cake will be seen in the local papers, on her news broadcast and by her over two hundred fifty guests. It might not sound like a lot, but in a town that only has one thousand residents, it means a lot.

I practically skip to the front of the bakery. Tina is cleaning off the small tables we have sitting in the front room. It's almost closing time, and she likes to be able to leave as soon as the doors lock.

"Hey Joy," Sam the delivery guy says, handing the package.

"Hey, Sam. Are you staying busy?"

"It's that time of year," he laughs. "Tina says you've been waiting for this little beauty," he adds, waving the box he just carried in.

I grab it from him, smiling ear to ear. I try to tear it open and quickly realize I'm going to need something to cut this damn packing tape with.

"What do they use to make this tape stick so good?" I grumble, taking the box to the counter and grabbing a pair of shears to slice through the it.

"Have no idea, but you're not the first to ask," he laughs.

"I wish I knew. I'd use it to invent a new type of spanks to help shrink my ass."

"Nothing wrong with your ass, Joy. From where I'm standing it's damn fine."

"Awe, Sam. You're so good for my ego. If you were just—"

"A few years younger?" he jokes, interrupting me.

"I was going to say single," I answer, shaking my head with a giggle. "How is Lani and the kids?"

"Beautiful and spoiled…. And the kids aren't bad either," he answers. "Oh hell. Is that what I think it is?" Sam asks from behind me.

I turn around holding up the contents of the delivery like a trophy. It's my Wayne Newton Christmas CD!

"I don't know Sam. What do you think it is?" I ask

"A CD? Do people actually use those things anymore?"

"Joy probably even has 8-tracks," Tina says sarcastically.

"Kiss my ass," I tell her, sticking out my tongue. I can't say too much because I actually do have an old one in my garage. It belonged to my dad. I even managed to keep an old CCR tape. "And besides," I continue, "This is not just any CD! It's the deluxe Wayne Newton's Christmas CD!"

"Wayne... *Newton?*" Sam repeats, like he doesn't believe me.

"Let her go, Sam. Just be thankful it's not Don Ho," Tina quips. I roll my eyes at her. I actually do have that one, but it's not as festive. Something about Wayne singing *"I'll Be Home for Christmas,"* never fails to get me in the Christmas spirit. Not that, that is too hard to do. Folks around down have nicknamed me Christmas Joy for a reason.

"On that note I'm out of here. You two have a great holiday if I don't see you again before then," Sam says, turning to leave.

"Wait!" I call. "I have something for you!"

"Now, Joy. As much as I joke, I am a married man."

"Very funny, Sam," I reply, shaking my head as I grab the red container and bring it to him. It's a large container covered in reindeers and the top says C&J Bakery.

"Is this cookies? Please tell me this is your Christmas cookies," Sam begs, making me grin.

"Cookies and peanut butter fudge. The cookies for your girls and the fudge is for you and Lani."

"You're an angel!" Sam grins, hugging me. "Have a great Christmas, Joy."

"You too." I watch him leave and then turn to look at Tina. "You think you can close? I want to run another container of cookies over to Mrs. Reynolds."

"I saw two containers," she replies.

"Yeah, I was going to take one to my new neighbor next door. He moved in three days ago and I still haven't met him. I thought it was the least I could do. I want to try and welcome him into the neighborhood."

"You haven't met him? That's a little strange."

"Yeah. I hope he's not an asshole. I'm already worried."

"Why? Does he have noisy pets or something? Women

coming and going all hours of the night? Give me the deets! You've been holding out on me."

"No. I mean well, I don't know. It's just that it's December now and Christmas is right around the corner…"

"Christmas?" Tina asks confused.

"Yeah and he's not put out one single decoration. It's downright depressing. When the Monroe family lived there they decked the place out. Actually my whole street decorates. This guy not decorating is making the house stick out like a sore thumb."

"Wait. If you haven't seen him, how do you know it's a man?"

"Lisa at the realtor office told me. He's supposed to be some kind of recluse. She said he was a writer, but she didn't recognize his name, so he must not be that great."

"Well, hey. Maybe he uses one of those pen names. You know?"

"Maybe," I shrug.

"Let me know if he's cute… Oh! And if he's single!" she says excitedly.

"Whatever. I don't really care what he is or isn't. I'm mostly hoping that getting a delivery of Christmas cookies, will give him the urge—"

"To sample other things you might offer him?" Tina giggles, trying to move her eyebrows back and forth. Sadly, she doesn't, so it mostly looks like she might need to go poop.

"To decorate his damn house! Or at least put up a tree! I just know he's going to cost my street the Juniper Springs County trophy this year for best décor!"

"The horror!" Tina mocks.

"I hate you. Just for that you're locking up completely on your own," I grumble. I put on my coat and then grab the two containers off the counter.

Tina just doesn't get it. Then again, most people don't understand my love of Christmas—which is sad.

It's the most wonderful time of the year! I giggle thinking of the old song and then I hum it as I make my way to the Senior Citizen's building at the end of town. Time to spread some cheer. At least Ms. Reynolds will appreciate it.

2

Eb

I rub the tension at the back of my neck. It's been a long fucking day. I'm working under a deadline. I need to have the first draft of this damn book finished in two weeks and the way things are going, there's no way that's going to happen. I had to be fucking insane to plan a move this close to my contractual obligations. I wish I had never signed that damn contract. There was a time writing was fun for me, but it's been so long ago I can barely remember it.

Now it's all about the Benjamins.

The thing about money is once you have a taste of the good life, you keep wanting more of it. It's a vicious damn cycle.

Still, today I seemed to have gotten in a groove. I've knocked out chapter after chapter and I'm actually liking the direction of the story. I'm typing away when... all at once I hear it.

Outside my window there's... *singing.* Several people singing actually, and at least two of them have to be completely tone deaf. All thought processes screech to a halt suddenly and as someone's voice cracks on Silent Night. Screech seems to be a good word to use. *Jesus.*

When I asked my agent to help find a rental that was in a

quiet town in Nowhere USA, I thought she had finally come through with Juniper Springs, Colorado. I should have been more specific, however. This whole place has gone Christmas crazy. My neighbor's decorations alone hurt my eyes to look at. I've had to have total blackout blinds installed and I swear there's still traces of light that seem to infiltrate my house. How the fuck they manage to pay their electric bill is beyond me. The place should be declared a national security risk. I'm pretty sure that there are planes above mistaking their yard for an airport runway, all because of the fucking lights.

I stand up, stretching muscles which are sore from lack of use. I don't know how many hours I've been sitting at my damn computer, but I'm pretty sure when I started that it was barely daylight. One glance at the clock tells me that night will be falling soon.

No wonder I'm fucking sore.

I might as well take a break and regroup since no more writing will be done today. I walk into the kitchen wondering if there is anything in here worth eating. I pull back the lid to the pizza I had delivered yesterday...or maybe a couple of days before. I can't really remember. When I'm writing I tend to get lost in the story and lose track of time. There's still a piece left and there's no mold on it, so I figure I'm good. I don't bother heating it up. Warmed up pizza is for men who shave their balls.

I walk back towards the front door, pizza in hand. As I go I'm sifting through my outline in my head, mentally going back through what I've written and trying to see where I still need to go. This is my process. It's also the reason why after I write a book that I do nothing for months afterwards—my brain needs a vacation. I open the door to check to see if the mailman left mail out front. The first couple of days he knocked. I don't remember him knocking today, but that doesn't mean he didn't. I trap the piece of pizza between my teeth and lips and open up the metal mailbox which is mounted beside the door. There's some mail in there, so I guess the guy did come by. I dig out the magazine and a few sales papers and one envelope. The only real mail seems to be a letter from my agent. I wasn't expecting one, so this could be good or bad. I take the last two bites of my pizza, tossing the leftover crust in a trashcan I keep by the entryway. I wipe my hand on my sweats, to rid it of at least some of the excess pizza sauce, and then I tear open the letter.

I read over the note, frowning because my balls are itching. Hearing from my agent has that effect on me. She's not bad to look at, but she has that hungry look about her that scares the shit out of me. Not the kind that says she's up for sex anytime and every time and will wear your dick out. The kind that says she'd chop your dick off if it meant she'd get further ahead. It's a scary fucking look for a woman, but a great one for an agent and the one simple reason I hired her. I move my hand down, sliding it between my stomach and sweats, scratching my balls, still reading the letter.

"Oh!"

A startled gasp comes from my left. I look over and see a sexy little blond holding a large container decorated in Christmas crap. She's wearing tight jeans that cling to her, an oversized white sweater, that sadly completely hides her tits from view, though I'm sure they are under there... *somewhere*. She also has some weird little Santa hat on that's red and complete with a white puffy ball on the end.

Suddenly I have the strangest urge to get on the naughty list.

3

Joy

I spent more time than I should have visiting Mrs. Reynolds, but she was lonesome. Still, as a result I'm really pushing it trying to get home before it gets dark. I don't normally drive, even in the colder weather. It just seems like a waste, because I don't live that far from town. But, now I'm really hoofing it to get home before dark. Juniper might be a quiet neighborhood, but a woman walking home alone after dark isn't safe anywhere these days. I turn the corner, deciding to go straight to my neighbor's house. I can deliver their package of Christmas cheer and hopefully help push him into the spirit and then go home and crash. I can already hear my large soaking tub calling my name. When I look up at my neighbor's door, my breath stops in my lungs.

He's standing at his mailbox, in sweats and he's not wearing a shirt and... *he's delicious.* That's the only word that comes to mind. *Delicious.* Because he is. He's like a Greek god—an Adonis in the flesh. His skin is a golden bronze, and looks so inviting... almost like candy because all you want to do is lick it. He's got wavy black hair that looks months too late for a cut, but the long, messy locks is sexy and screams with masculinity. There's traces of gray here and there, but that only makes it more appealing.

His face looks as if it was chiseled by an artist. It's just that perfect. He even has this perfectly symmetrical indention on his chin that makes me wonder what it would feel like to slide my tongue against it.

I find myself hoping he's single. I find myself praying he's the answer to the long dry spell I've been having.

I start to speak up to announce my presence when I see him move his hand inside his gym pants. I blush slightly, but even though I know I shouldn't—I still watch. He moves his hand down, adjusting himself and I swallow, because my throat is suddenly dry.

Then he does something that completely floors me.

His hand moves in his pants and I can see him actually stretching out his shaft. It's not hard—at least not completely—but, even through the loose sweatpants that he's wearing you can tell he's packing. He's big. *Really big.*

I can't stop the startled, "Oh!", that comes out of my mouth, or the way I feel flushed, weak, and yet strangely energized all at the same time.

He turns to face me then and I can feel heat fill my face. His gaze moves up and down my body. It lingers on my breasts and the look in his eyes excites me. I should be ashamed at the wetness gathering against my panties, but I'm not. It's been a long time since a man has looked at me and even then, he looked nothing like this man. This man is…

Sex on a stick.

"Hello," he says. That's it. Just one word, but his voice is deep, throaty, with a touch of playfulness in it and if my panties weren't already wet…

"Hi. Um… I didn't mean to bother you," I answer. I start off in a whisper, my vocal chords not exactly wanting to work. But, to be fair, it's hard to tell what I sound like over the pounding of my heart.

"Honey you're no bother. You're a dream come true," he says with a quick, dirty, little grin. I really should dismiss his words—maybe even run back home. I can't seem to make myself do either of those.

"Um…" I stutter, because I have no idea what to say to that. He's probably making fun of me. I'm used to that. Folks in town are good to me, and most like me. Still, how many times have I heard them laugh about Christmas Joy?

Maybe I shouldn't have worn the Santa hat?

"I brought you a gift. A welcome to the neighborhood kind of thing," I tell him lamely, stepping in closer to him. I'm proud of myself that I manage not to stare as he pulls his hand out of his pants.

"Is it you? Because if so, I need to give my realtor a bonus for finding this house."

"I uh… What? No," I answer, completely flustered now. "I made you some cookies… you know… for Christmas," I answer —rather lamely.

"Isn't that a coincidence," he says, bending his head to lean down closer to me. He's so tall. *So. Impossibly. Tall.* And big. *So. Epically. Big.*

"It is?" I ask, biting my lip trying to remember if I've ever seen eyes like his before. They look like warm caramel.

"I was just wondering what your cookie would taste like," he says and I've not dealt with many men before. I've had a boyfriend here or there, but my business always came first. This is the first man I've met that makes me feel like that might have been a mistake. Still, I get the feeling when he says cookie, he's not talking about the ones I've baked and a shiver runs through me.

"I… they're traditional sugar cookies," I tell him, trying to get control of the conversation again.

"I knew they'd taste sweet," he answers, grinning. He finally takes the box into his hand. The very hand he had wrapped around his cock. *Jesus.*

"My name is Joy. I run the local bakery in town. Comfort and Joy?" I tell him, at this point feeling like I'm blathering on like an idiot.

"Nice play on Christmas," he says, studying me closely and this time I can't really guess what he's thinking.

"That was the thought. I'm kind of a Christmas freak."

"Is that a fact?"

"Yeah. It's kind of a running joke in town. They call me Christmas Joy, because I like to go around and spread the Christmas cheer…"

"Spread…"

"Anyway, I know moving can be hectic and things. I'm right next door if you'd like help getting moved in or maybe putting up your Christmas decorations or whatever. I'm your girl."

"You certainly are," he says and his voice is so intense, I step back on reflex.

"Well, I… I guess I should go. Remember my offer," I tell him, feeling like a fool. I back away and he turns to watch me with a big grin on his face. I literally back all the way to my yard.

"Trust me, Joy. I'm not about to forget your offer," he says and those shivers I've been feeling intensify all at once.

For some reason, that felt like a warning…

4

Eb

I hate Christmas. I always have. My grandmother used to say my parents jinxed me by making my middle name Eben. She hated it and always said it was too close to Ebenezer. I didn't really give a fuck, though I found myself glad I didn't pack around the name Ebenezer my whole life. That would suck fucking ass. I'm not too fond of Eben, but I also don't spend much time thinking about it.

I write under the name E.B. Mason and that name I like, because that name makes money and really that's the only thing that matters. I need to go finish my book, but little Joy has me wishing I could do something else. Her, actually. She's a hot little package and I bet she'd be sweet as hell to sink into. She wouldn't put up much of a fight either. She was practically begging to be fucked right here on my doorstep. I have the urge to tie her up and make her beg me to fuck her. That idea is infinitely more appealing than going back to writing.

Maybe I could take a few days off? I mean I have a deadline, but my brain is fried. It's Christmas. Everyone deserves a little time off. It doesn't matter that I hate the holiday. I mean I do hate everything about it, but that's not important right now. I don't hate my new neighbor. Hell, I'm liking so much about her, I'm willing to ignore her love of this god awful holiday. Who knows? Maybe she could make me change my mind. If she fucks as good as she looks…

I find myself grinning. I need a hook. I don't have a lot of time, and I can't afford to waste much on my hot neighbor. She definitely seems like she needs a good fuck, and that's half the battle. She wants to help me decorate for Christmas? I can let her decorate her little heart out and then after I make sure she leaves my bed crying out, *O' holy night,* I'll get back to work.

That seems simple. And my cock is rock hard imagining it.

I go back inside, closing my door, still thinking about it. I go back to my computer, but for once, I ignore my manuscript. Instead, I find myself searching lingerie. Lingerie for a certain little blond neighbor that I'm going to enjoy putting on the naughty list. I know exactly what I'm looking for and almost laugh out loud when I find it. Sexy little red and white silk, barely-there, corset, panties and matching garters. If Santa was real, this is exactly what he'd make Mrs. Claus wear to their bed.

She likes Christmas? I can definitely make that work for me. And I definitely know that this Christmas, for once, I'm going to enjoy *spreading* Christmas Joy.

Fuck yeah I will.

5

Joy

I come awake with a start. I look over at the clock, my eyes blurry with sleep. It's seven in the morning... on a Sunday. Two days after I've made a fool of myself in front of my new neighbor, and two days in which he still hasn't put up one trace of a decoration. It's a silly thing really, but ever since I moved into my house our street has won the annual Christmas trophy. At this point, it's a source of pride. There's no way we will win this year—not with my neighbor's house being completely undecorated. There might be bigger problems in this world, but it makes me sad.

My doorbell rings again and I remember why I woke in the first place. I look again at the clock.

Who even gets up at seven in the morning on a Sunday?!?!

It's my one day of the week to be sloth-Joy. I stand up, shivering without the covers as the cool air of the house hits me. I look mournfully at my sheets and favorite blanket as my doorbell goes off again.

"Alright! Hang on! Keep your pants on!" I grumble. There's a terrible secret about me that no one knows. I may love Christmas and everything about it, but there's nothing cheerful and joyful about me in the mornings. I have to have at least two cups of coffee before any of the real me starts shining through. I grab my ratty old robe off the side of my bed, wrapping it around me like a security blanket. It's warm cotton, and at one time I think it was a vibrant red. It's so old and has been washed so many times it's a pale pink now.

I look through the peephole, and I have to hold onto the door to keep from falling.

My neighbor is outside! My sexy neighbor is outside my house at seven in the morning looking freaking amazing and, and…

And shit! I'm here without my hair brushed, in my ratty old robe, and I probably have morning breath! *Shit!*

I push my hand through my hair, trying to comb it with my fingers. I'm positive it doesn't, but at least I tried. I try to make a mental note not to breathe on him, or talk a lot just in case he might be able to smell my breath. I paste on a fake smile and then I open the door—all while searching for something cool and fun to say.

"Um… hi," I say and bang the side of my head gently against the door, wondering what it is about this man that makes my brains go as limp as a wet noodle.

"Hey Christmas Joy. You're looking pretty this morning," he says—obviously lying through his perfect, white teeth. Good gravy, how does one get teeth that perfect? Are they fake? I doubt anything on this man is fake.

"Hey… umm…"

"Eb."

"Eb?"

"That's my name," he says, laughing.

"Oh… I'm Joy."

"Yeah. You are."

I'm wishing the ground would swallow me up. *Is that really so much to ask?*

"Why are you here?" I ask, and I wouldn't have thought it was possible, but now I feel even more stupid.

"Is your offer still open?"

I really can't think this early. I'm racking my brain trying to figure out I offered him. As stupid as I go around him, I might have offered to wash his body… *with my tongue.*

"Um…"

"If it's not, that's totally fine, it's just I could really use Christmas Joy's help," he says, looking like a sad little puppy who lost his favorite chew toy.

Those eyes… those damn eyes of his.

"What offer?" I ask, drowning in deep pools of caramel.

"To help me decorate?" he asks and my heart speeds up.

"You want to decorate your house?" I question, shock coloring my voice.

"Well, everyone else is, I thought maybe I should."

"For Christmas?" I add, like a fool.

"Is there another holiday I don't know about?"

"Um… No. No, that's the only one."

God. I'm such a dummy.

"Then, yes. Definitely for Christmas."

"I want to help!" I practically shout.

"I was hoping." He laughs and he must think I'm a loon after all of this, but instead of making me feel worse, he gives this smile that reaches those caramel eyes of his and I feel like a big melted pool of goo.

"What did you have in mind?" I ask, and for the first time in a long time, Christmas is not what I'm thinking about.

"I was hoping you could go shopping with me and help pick out my decorations and…"

"And a tree?"

"A tree?" he asks, clearly surprised.

"You have to have a Christmas tree!"

"I do?"

"A big one! You have those amazing windows in the front of your house. A big tree would look awesome there.

"It would?" he asks, and I think I've shell-shocked him.

"Definitely. If you give me a bit to get ready, we can go to town today," I tell him, suddenly very excited.

"That sounds good," he says, but his voice sounds more reserved than earlier. For some reason I think he might be hesitant on getting a tree. Surely that can't be it? Maybe he just doesn't want a big one? Some people like small trees or even porcelain ones. The thought that Eb might be like that makes me sad. Hopefully, I can steer him the right way with a little work.

"I'll get ready and come to your house in about an hour. Is that okay?"

"That sounds great," he whispers, and he brings his finger up to touch along the side of my face.

It's by sheer willpower alone that I bite into my lip and don't move my mouth to suck his finger.

Sheer-freaking-willpower.

This may be a long day.

6

Eb

Shit, Joy has some fucking amazing tits. I couldn't see them yesterday, but today they are up close and personal. She's wearing jeans and another sweater today, this one gray, but it has a V-neck and every time she moves it dips into the valley of these perfect C-cup tits. They make me want to bury my head in them like a kid diving for apples. That view alone is enough to make this entire shopping torture worth it.

And then there are moments like this...

"Joy? What do you think about this?" I ask, leaning over to look at the most horribly, obscene tree I can find. It's only about a foot tall, made entirely of pink foil and clearly hidden at the bottom of a shelf on purpose.

For some unknown reason, Joy has made it her life's mission to help me find a Christmas tree. I don't want a tree. When I decided to seduce little Miss Christmas Joy out of her Christmas cookies—so to speak—I felt it was a big enough concession to have shit littering my lawn. There was no way I wanted the decorating to infiltrate my house. I was going to tell her hell no. Then, the strangest thing happened.

I enjoyed my time with her. It was fun watching her get so

hyped up about the decorations and I'm finding myself having fun. What's even better, are times like this.

Joy moves in front of me and leans over to look at the sad little fake tree.

First my gaze goes to her tits, because if I angle my head just right, I can see her tits in that pale pink silk bra she's wearing. It's a damn good view and I love the way her tits are doing their best to get out of the bra. Overfilling the cups is a real thing and definitely a great problem for Joy to have. Still, *even that* isn't as great as what comes next.

My gaze slowly travels down her back to her ass. She's leaning over to look at the shelf. And she's in the perfect position for me to fuck her doggy style. Those jeans are stretched across that juicy ass and it's enough to make a man beg. I can't tear my eyes away. To be honest, her ass is just that good.

"Damn that's a nice view. Am I right?" I look beside me to see another man, his gaze trained on Joy's ass and I don't like it. It's okay for me to look at her ass. Hell, I've been having her bend over the whole day to look at shit, for that sole reason.

It's not okay for another man to be looking at her ass. It's not that I'm territorial—or rather I haven't been before. It's just the fact, that this is the ass I've now invested time in and an ass I'm definitely going to tap and therefore… *mine.*

"Look elsewhere," I growl, keeping my voice quiet, so Joy doesn't hear us talking.

"Are you crazy? There's nothing in this fucking store even close to that view. Damn a man would give his right nut to come home to that ass every night," the guy says a little too loudly.

Luckily, Joy has no idea because she's busy talking about the shelf being overcrowded and not seeing what I'm talking about. To quickly end this conversation, I hit this asshole in the stomach. When he starts to bitch, I hit him hard in the mouth and he goes back with a thud.

"Oh my God! What happened?" Joy asks, standing up and that's another reason to hate this bastard. I didn't get to enjoy her ass longer. People go around the man who is now lying on the floor—moaning, but that's about it.

"Some guy passed out, hit his face on the way down," I shrug. "I think I'd rather have a real tree," I invent to distract her as I steer her away. I don't really want to explain why I knocked the guy out and if he starts spouting shit again, I can't be responsible for what I might do to him.

"Oh, okay…" Joy says looking over her shoulder at the man. Finally, she turns to look at me. A live tree is a great idea and they smell divine. Besides…" she stops with a frown, her face studying me. "You can't have that tree, Eb."

"I can't?"

"No. It's hideous and I say that with love. There is not one redeeming thing about that tree."

"It's made out of recyclable material," I offer, feeling helpful.

"From what? An explosion at the Hello, Kitty factory?"

Her response makes me laugh. Again, it surprises me how much I really like being around her. She's funny and cute, which is a strange combination when her body is made for sin.

I look at my watch and try to hide my smile.

"So, I guess we're saying no to the trees right now, because the lot will be closed since it's Sunday." I tell her, slightly relieved.

"I guess so," she sighs almost sounding broken hearted and making me feel guilty for not picking one of the fifty that she showed me. "I haven't given up hope that eventually we will find one we can agree on. At least we got some lights and lawn decorations."

"At least there's that," I answer, feeling sad that my lawn is going to look like Santa's sleigh vomited on it. "I'm hungry. You feel like grabbing some lunch before we go back and start decorating?" I suggest.

I want to spend more time with her and there's the added

bonus that I really should eat now. If I wait until all that crap has to be put up in my yard, I'll probably lose my appetite.

"I'd really like that," she answers, smiling at me. She's got dimples. I hadn't noticed those before. And, her eyes sparkle a bright, deep blue that reminds me of the water in Cabo, and in that moment I almost like her eyes more than her ass.

It might be time to start worrying about little Miss Christmas Joy.

7

Joy

I can't believe what a great time I'm having with Eb. He's funny and attentive and he keeps touching me. It's nothing really out of the way. He puts his hand on my back as we walk, he brushes hair from my face, or he holds my hand. I've never had a man be this attentive before. It makes me feel... *special.*

I was delighted he asked me out to eat. I really didn't want our time together to end. We walk to the local café and we find a small table by a window. Outside the window is a huge juniper tree that the city has decorated. I watch the lights twinkling and smile.

"You really love this Christmas shit, don't you?" Eb asks and he sounds surprised. I turn to look at him in shock.

"It's the most wonderful time of the year," I answer, laughing. "Don't you like it?" I ask him after a little bit of silence. I'm confused, if he doesn't actually like Christmas then I don't understand why I am here.

"Of course I do," he says, looking around the café. If I didn't there'd be no reason for you to decorate for me... right?" he says, his gaze coming back to me.

"Right," I tell him, but I feel like I'm missing something in this conversation. There's like a strange undercurrent that I'm not grasping.

The waitress comes and takes our order and I try my best to shake it off. Today has been so great, I'm sure I'm just being silly.

"I hate that we didn't find a tree, but your yard is going to look so pretty! Our street will definitely win the annual trophy!"

"Trophy?" Eb asks.

"The city of Juniper gives out a trophy every year to the street with the best decorations."

"Who gets the trophy?"

"They have it on display at City Hall for everyone to see. Our street has a history of winning it," I tell him proudly.

"There's no money reward? You do it for a trophy?"

"Of course! It's a pride kind of thing," I tell him with a silly smile as the waitress serves our food.

"Is that why you offered to decorate my yard? To win the trophy, I mean," Eb questions me.

I push my food around in the plate and then look over at him.

"Yeah. Honestly, if you don't decorate we will never win and we always win…"

"I see. So it's really important to you that my yard looks like Santa puked on it?"

I blink at his description.

"Santa puked? Eb you don't really sound like you like Christmas at all. Why are you doing all this if you don't?" I ask him earnestly, trying to understand what exactly is going on.

8

Eb

I sit there for a moment and wonder exactly what will happen with Joy if I tell her the simple truth.

Dear, sweet Christmas Joy, I'm only doing this so I can get in your pants.

Somehow I don't think her reaction would get me where I want—which is between her legs. I have two clear paths in front of me. One has a very good chance of getting me laid and the other will probably dash all hopes quicker than Santa's sleigh in fresh snow.

There's a moment in every man's life when he comes to a crossroads. Now I could tell her the truth and if that kept me out from between Joy's legs... *so be it.* I mean she's hot and has this innocent vibe about her that I really like. She looks so innocent and pure that I can't help but want to dirty her up.

Still, I've never had to chase pussy in my life and I'm a little too fucking old and jaded to start now. I mean giving a girl my name these days usually assures my cock is going to get sucked. And, as delectable and little Joy appears to be, in the end she's still a warm, wet pussy to sink into. It's not like this is love. I don't believe in that shit anyhow.

I've almost decided to pull the plug on this little endeavor when Joy does something that changes the game. Something I didn't really expect.

Joy reaches over and drags the pad of her finger across the indention on my chin. It's a simple touch and there's nothing sexual about it, but then she smiles at me. It's a sweet smile, almost shy and it's definitely tender. I grew up with my father, who was strictly military. My mother died when I was barely three. I don't really remember her and I can never remember tenderness. Joy gave me tenderness just now and I find myself wanting that more—or almost more—than getting between her legs.

"You look like you're making a life or death decision, Eb," she says softly and it must be said that I like the way she says my name. I want her to say it more… *a lot more.*

"Sometimes when you smile, I look at you and lose track of what I'm doing," I tell her and for once, I'm not feeding a girl a line. I'm being completely upfront with her.

Shock moves over her face and I can literally see it. Her eyes go round in surprise and she blushes.

"I was telling you that it feels like you don't really like Christmas and I can't understand why you asked me to help you, if you don't."

"I love Christmas," I tell her—lying through my fucking teeth.

"You do?"

"And I can honestly tell you Joy that with you involved, I'm liking Christmas more and more."

"Really?"

"Absolutely. I was actually dreading this Christmas before I met you Joy. I owe you for helping me find the old Christmas spirit."

"Now you're just making things up."

"Nope. I'm being completely truthful. Scout's honor."

"Were you ever a scout, Eb?" she asks with a smile.

"Once a very long time ago," I tell her, even though the memory is not a good one, I don't let her in on that sad truth.

"Well then, I'm going to make it my job to bring you all the Christmas joy I can."

"I can hardly wait," I say with a grin. "I'm dying for more of Christmas Joy." I tell her, and even though I figure we're talking about two very different things, I still feel like I just scored the winning touchdown.

Joy has no idea what's in store for her.

9

Joy

"Want to come back to my place? We could have a nightcap, watch a movie…" Eb asks, his full lips stretching into a smile that looks inviting, but also reminds me of a wolf getting ready to devour its prey.

My legs go weak and it feels like I have to push air through my lungs. He wraps a strand of my hair around his fingers, his dark gaze following the movement. I moisten my lips with my tongue, trying to find my voice. I really want to say yes, but I barely know Eb and I have a feeling if I took him up on his offer —I wouldn't be leaving until morning.

"I better not, I have to work early in the morning," I answer, my voice a mixture of breathless excitement and nerves. "If I don't get to bed early, I'll oversleep," I add, clearly rattling.

"You could grab your pajamas and come stay with me. I'll make sure you get in bed *really* early."

"Uh—"

"I'll even make sure you get up early too."

"I'm not sure we know each other enough for me to take you up on that offer," I answer, and I have to force the words out of my mouth. I really don't want to tell him no, even if it is the wisest thing to do.

"If you come home with me, we'll definitely get to know each other much better."

"Are you trying to seduce me, Eb?" I ask, because I know he is. It's just a shock that he's coming on so strong after a fun and flirty day.

"Could I?"

"Probably…" I whisper, as his head drops closer to mine. "In time…"

"Kiss me, Joy," he says right before his lips touch mine.

There's something about the taste of a man's lips, the elemental flavor when they invade your mouth that I've always liked. I've not kissed a lot of men, but each one has been different, unique. Some I have liked. Some I never wanted to repeat and one or two that have kept in my memory. I'm thirty years old and I don't think I've ever tasted a man's kiss that made me want to moan from the beginning. And, it's not just his taste. It's the growl he emits as he devours me. The forcefulness of his hold on me and the way he takes charge. It's all of that combined and more. In all of my thirty years, I've never been exposed to someone as masculine as Eb.

When we finally break apart, I have to lean on him until my legs can hold me up once again. His fingers are biting into my skin, but I like it. There will probably be bruises on my hips where he's holding me and I find I don't care at all.

"Last chance beautiful," he says and it might be my imagination, but I think his voice is filled with hunger.

"I…" I war with myself. I want to say yes, but I've learned that snap decisions are not good—especially when it involves romance. I've been burned before and I'm not ready to go down that road again. "I better not," I whisper instead and it's surprising how much those words hurt.

He pulls away with a frown. He walks backwards a few steps, his gaze appraising me.

"You know where I am, Christmas Joy," he responds and then turns around and leaves. I stand there looking at him, watching until he makes it to his house and closes the front door.

Sadness fills me, along with a feeling that I've made a mistake…

10

Eb

I may have outplayed this little endeavor. I'm never had a problem getting a woman underneath me. Usually my fame, pocketbook, and the fact my books hit the New York Times Bestseller list on a regular basis do that for me. Joy is different. She didn't ask one damn thing about my writing, not over dinner and not throughout the day. We talked about a million things, but none of them revolved around my work. I didn't realize that until the night came to an end. I have no idea what it means.

I probably know more about Joy after our day together than I've known about any other woman in my life, which is fucking weird.

I know she owns her own bakery, loves Christmas, and decorates her trees in themes every year. I know that this year the theme is old fashioned snowmen and last year it was Santa. I know she loves to bake, but hates cooking. I know she will be alone this Christmas because her sister is out of town to her fiancé's family, and they usually spend Christmas together. Hell, I even know that her favorite color is red and her favorite tree is a Holly tree.

This is all useless information that for some reason I took in today, because… I liked her. I even talked about myself, which is something I've never done much of. I don't share myself with others easily—it's different with Joy for some reason.

Still, I don't need to tie myself up in knots over a girl and I don't have time to invest in a long term thing. Today was good, but without a reward I don't need to waste the effort. I have a damn deadline looming over my head.

I stare at my laptop. I could write, but I'm not feeling it tonight. I'll take a shower, clear my head of all things Joy and start fresh tomorrow.

It sounds like an excellent plan, but when I get there even the hot water and steam fails to remove Joy from my mind. The feel of the water moving over my skin just makes me think more about her. Drying off, I imagine her drying me.

Christ. I need to get laid. I've been without a woman for far too long and for some reason Joy has started a fire in my blood. One that apparently she's not willing to quench. Damn her.

I toss and turn for a few minutes and curse all things Christmas and blond women everywhere when I decide to quit fighting it. I flop to my back and grab my cock in my hand, closing my eyes and picturing Joy between my legs with those thick, lush, wet lips about to slide down on my cock and devour me.

I'll make her swallow every drop for punishment.

Joy

I'm insane... or maybe bipolar. I can't believe I'm doing this. Especially since I've had one date with the man. Actually, I'm not sure you can call the day we've shared a date. Eh, it doesn't matter either way. I'm going to his house to get laid after one non-date first date. Pretty sure that equates to me being one of those scarlet women my grandmother used to talk about with her church friends, while shaking her head and clicking her tongue in disgust.

Luckily, grandmother is long gone and will never know her granddaughter is one of those fallen women. Of course she never liked me much either and now I'm probably going to hell for loose morals and thinking it's good she's dead. I guess I'll see her again after all.

I stop raging a war with my brain when I come to Eb's door. He didn't close it. It's pulled together, but not shut, there's about a two-inch crack. Surely he didn't mean to do that. It can be dangerous and his electric bill will skyrocket. He can't mean to heat all of the outdoors. I frown at that thought, because now I'm even starting to sound like my grandmother.

I tighten my hands into fists a few times, trying to gather

together my courage and then I knock on the door. I look, but I don't see a doorbell. I wait for him to show up, or at least yell a response but a few minutes pass and there's nothing. I knock again. *Still nothing.* I know he's here, maybe he's done with me since I just turned him down. Not that he knows this is me. I don't think he could—unless there's a camera around here. I look around trying to spot a security camera. How embarrassing would it be if Eb is watching me from his computer and laughing because I turned him down, but changed my mind. I frown, when I don't see a camera or anything. I start to turn around, but instead I knock one last time. I need to get a grip. Maybe he was just in the restroom or something. He could be asleep, which is just another reason the door should have been closed and locked. Eb could be murdered or anything with his door open like that while trying to sleep. I start to pull it closed and then freeze. Images of Eb, lying in a pool of blood, bludgeoned to death by a hammer, which is lying close to his lifeless body, flash through my mind.

I watch way too many true crime shows, but still I am panicking. Before I can second guess myself I push his door open the rest of the way and walk through.

His house is dark. I use my hands to pat the wall, finding a light switch. Pale light floods the room. There's a desk with a computer on it, and it looks like sticky notes have exploded all over the room. There is, however, not one sign of a murder or break in.

I start to back out of the room and run to my house, before Eb finds me and decides to call the police on me for breaking into his house. Then, I hear a moan. It's faint but clearly a moan. I take a hesitant step forward when I hear it again. Now those visions of Eb's bloody death come back to me and I walk hesitantly toward them. I see the canister of cookies I brought the other day, sitting on the edge of the desk. As self-defense goes it sucks, but I grab it. Maybe I can throw it at him and distract him enough to get away if he turns his knife on me.

I feel like I'm walking on hot coals as I make it to the last door at the end of the hall. I hear small undisguisable noises coming from in there. I reach out to open the cracked door a little more, while simultaneously trying to talk myself out of it so I can run away. Just as I'm about to turn the knob I hear Eb again. It's his voice and I know a moment of joy because he's obviously alive.

"Yes," he moans out and it's definitely a moan. I open the door thinking of nothing more than the fact that Eb's alive, but he's moaning. Maybe he fell... "Joy," he growls and I open the door.

My eyes go round. My mouth drops open.

Eb is lying on the bed with his hand wrapped around his cock. A very large cock that is hard and glistening. He's stroking himself and his head is thrown back against the pillow. He's jacking himself off and from the looks of things he's very close.

He's jacking himself off.

And it's my name he growled.

Mine.

Oh boy...

12

Eb

God. I haven't jacked-off into my own hand in fucking years, but with visions of Joy floating in my head, sucking my cock, I can feel cum rising in my balls. I'm so close to exploding, I just need one little push over the edge. I throw my head back and close my eyes tight, conjuring up a picture of Joy bound to my bed, her legs stretched apart to the point their almost painful, her pussy glistening with her juices, and begging for my tongue.

I'm so lost in the fantasy I can smell Joy now. That scent of sugar and vanilla that's oh so sweet it makes me hungry to taste her. Fuck, what I wouldn't give to have her body to paint with my...

"Eb..."

My body jerks. That wasn't part of the dream I'm playing in my head. My hand tightens on my dick as I stop mid-stroke. I look up to see Joy standing at my door, her gaze is glued on my dick and she's licking her lips.

Fuck yes.

"See something you like?" I ask, my voice hoarse, throaty even and full of hunger.

"I... I thought you were hurt," she whispers, but she still

doesn't tear her gaze away from my dick. I stroke myself again, just to see what she does. I can literally here her take a shuddering breath as her hand comes up against her chest.

"I am hurt."

"You are?" she asks and finally she looks at my face.

"I'm in a lot of pain, sweet Joy."

"I… you are?" she asks again, her eyes round and she's biting down on her bottom lip and something about the way I can see a hint of her teeth against the lush red lips is fucking sexy.

"I'm so fucking hard it hurts, Joy. I need your help."

"You… Eb, I… *shit,*" she whispers.

Her whispered curse makes me hungry. I want to make her say all kinds of bad, bad words. Somehow, I think they'd be fucking hot coming from her lips.

"Take off your clothes, Joy. Come make me all better," I tell her, smiling. I hold my hand at the base of my cock and squeeze it, trying to calm myself down. Now that Joy is here, I can't shoot my load too soon. I need to wait… *until I can paint Joy in my cum and make her beg for more.*

"I shouldn't."

"You're here for a reason, Joy," I growl, I won't let her back out.

"Your door was open. You could have been attacked. I came here to help," she says lamely.

"And you were going to what?"

"To try and stop them so they wouldn't hurt you," she says, shaking the tin of cookies she gave me the other day.

Her gaze has gone back to my cock so I stroke it, hoping that will keep her from trying to back out. Pre-cum slides from the head of my cock and down my shaft and over my hand. God when I come, I'm going to drown her in it.

"Take your clothes off, Joy. Let me give you what those pretty blue eyes of yours are begging for."

"I shouldn't," she says, but she starts unbuttoning her coat.

She lets it fall to the ground and then lifts her shirt over her head. She holds the fabric in front of her for a minute and then lets it fall too.

"But you're going to," I respond.

"But I'm going to," she softly murmurs as she unzips her pants.

13

Joy

Good sense was thrown out the window when I walked in and saw Eb stroking himself. Until that moment, I didn't think a man could be beautiful, but that private moment I witnessed with Eb was a thing of beauty. One that blew all of the reasons why this was a bad idea, out of the water. Besides, there's no point in pretending. I came over here because I wanted Eb. I could color it up and make the reasons why pretty, but it wouldn't change the truth. And the truth is raw and dirty.

I want to feel Eb between my legs. I want to feel him deep inside of me. From looking at his huge cock with the broad head that's wet with his desire, there's no way I'm leaving until I get that. Until I have every inch of him.

I practically hold my breath as the last of my clothes fall to the floor.

"Climb up on the bed," Eb orders. His voice is huskier than normal, full of need.

I have a moment of fear, or maybe it's embarrassment. Eb seems to understand because he reaches his hand out, rolling to his side, and pulling me into him.

"You're warm," I murmur, somewhat lamely.

39

"There's no need to be nervous, sweetheart. I'm going to make you feel good. I'm going to make us both feel good."

"I know, it's just I haven't done this before," I assure him, blushing.

"You're a virgin?"

"What? No," I answer, feeling more embarrassed. "But I've always been in a relationship. I've never done this with a stranger before."

"We're not strangers, Joy."

"I don't think one date makes us friends, Eb."

"That's where you are wrong, Joy," he responds, taking my hand and guiding it to the base of his cock. He's so big and thick that my hand doesn't completely wrap around it. "We're about to get very friendly."

"With what you are packing, if we get too friendly, I won't be able to walk afterwards," I tell him. I'm not really joking, but Eb gives a soft laugh. It's a good sound and for some reason it calms me like nothing else could.

I leave my worries behind. I may not have known Eb for very long, but being with him is comfortable, it feels right. That truth emblazons me. It makes me bold.

I tighten my hand on his cock and instantly Eb groans. I keep the pressure and stroke him from root to tip and just as I get to the head, I curl my hand to one side. Eb exhales with a rumbling noise and his hips thrust toward me.

"Fuck, Joy."

"You like that?" I ask, smiling. Sliding my hand back down his shaft.

"I think you're teasing me Joy. Do you know what happens when you tease?"

"Wha-t?"

My question comes out broken with a moan mixed in some-where in the middle, because Eb slides his fingers between the lips of my pussy. They brush against the sensitive skin, sending electrical charges of desire through me. He stokes against my clit, before pushing hard against it. I whimper, trying to tighten my legs around his hand to ride. He moves his fingers in a small half-moon shape clockwise and then counter-clockwise, playing my body like an instrument.

He repeats his movements over and over all while kissing me and swallowing my cries. Finally, he pulls away so I can take oxygen into my body, but I whimper, because I already miss him. His lips make a slow trail down my neck and chest. When his lips latch onto one of my nipples, he thrusts his fingers deep inside of me, and my body comes up off the bed.

"You're soaked, Joy, but still so fucking tight. Your little cunt is squeezing my fingers. Do you think you will be able to take all of me inside of you?" he asks. Then, he somehow stretches me. I can feel his fingers drag and press against my inner walls and I can do nothing more than moan his name.

"Eb, please."

"Please what?"

"I need you inside of me," I beg. My voice comes out harsher, almost to the point that it sounds more like a demand.

In answer, Eb takes his fingers and his mouth away, lying on his back. I lift up looking down at him, afraid he is going to stop and that's the last thing I want.

He grins at me and then brings his fingers to his mouth. They are slick and glossy with my juices. I start to beg him for more when he wraps his tongue around his fingers and then sucks my wetness from them.

"You taste so good. I loved the Christmas cookies you brought over, but I think my favorite flavor of the season is Christmas Joy."

"Quit teasing me."

He reaches over to his nightstand and pulls open a small drawer. He grabs a condom and dangles it in front of me.

"Put it on me," he orders, his voice dark and demanding. It sends shivers down my spine. I take it from him, my gaze holding his. I love the look on his face and the way the dark color in his eyes seems to intensify. I put the foil wrapper in my mouth and tear it open. "That's my girl," he says with a smile. His thumb comes up to brush the corner of my mouth and I feel like stretching with pride.

I like that. *I want to be his girl.*

I take my time sliding the condom down his thick cock and each time his fingers bite into my hips, all while thrusting into my hand, I feel pride. When I'm done, I stare at how tight the latex is on his shaft. I'm actually surprised it holds him. I must stare for a little too long. Eb slaps the side of my ass to get my attention.

"Ow," I whisper, still grinning, because it didn't hurt.

"On your knees and guide me inside of you, Joy."

"You're so bossy," I chastise.

"You haven't seen nothing yet, honey. Take me inside of you," he urges again.

I hold his cock, brushing his shaft against my clit. I whimper at how good that small movement feels. Then, I position him at my entrance. I slowly lower down on him, hissing at the way he stretches me with every inch I take.

"So fucking good," Eb growls, and then he takes over, grabbing my hips and pulling me down on him quickly. When he's all the way inside, I have to catch my breath. Eb has his eyes closed and he slowly opens them and the look on his face feels almost like a physical touch.

"Eb…" I whisper his name, so full of emotion, I'm not sure what I want to say.

"Ride me, Joy. Take us both to heaven," he orders, his voice dark, vibrating and so commanding I do it without question.

Then again, I need him so much I don't have a choice. I've got to have more.

I have a feeling when it comes to Eb, I will always want more.

14

Joy

"Morning, sleepyhead," I laugh when Eb comes into the kitchen scratching the back of his head. His hair is all ruffled from sleep and he's wearing nothing but jeans. Eb has an amazing body, his chest covered in a light layer of chest hair, his skin golden in color and abs that men would envy and women would beg to touch—or lick.

"Who gave you permission to get out of bed?" He grumbles with a yawn, his big hand moving against his chest, scratching through the hair.

Definitely sexy.

"I wanted to fix you breakfast, before I had to leave," I tell him, giggling as he wraps his arms around me and snuggles into my back. He kisses my neck, biting it tenderly enough that tiny chills of excitement run through me.

"Who said you can leave?" he grumbles, his hot breath exciting me further.

"I have to get to work sweetheart."

"Take the day off."

His hand moves up to palm my breasts, squeezing them

gently. My knees weaken as I try to concentrate on stirring the scrambled eggs so they don't burn.

"It's one of the busiest days at the bakery," I try and explain, my voice soft and full of need. "I have to work. I should have already left, but I wanted to make sure you ate breakfast before you got lost in your work."

"How do you know I get lost in my work?" Eb asks me, surprise lacing his voice. He stops massaging my breasts, but he keeps his hand on them—possessively.

"Because you left the bed at three this morning to go work on your computer."

"You were awake? I thought I wore you out enough with round three that you were dead to the world."

"I was awake, but I figured you wanted to work, so I just went back to sleep. Now quit teasing me, so I can get your breakfast on the table before I leave."

I'm almost sad when he does as I asked, and leaves me to sit at the small table in the corner of the kitchen. I put his food on a plate and then place it in front of him. He stares at it a moment and I start to panic. *Did I mess something up?*

I hate cooking, it's true. Cooking is nothing like baking for me. Baking for some reason I find pretty and it feeds my creativity. The same will never be said about cooking—at least not for me. Still, I'm not horrible at it. I didn't fix anything horrible. It's just bacon, eggs and toast. So his silence makes me feel unsure.

"Where's yours?"

"I don't really eat breakfast," I shrug uncomfortably.

"So, you just fixed breakfast for me?"

"I thought it would give you energy so you could work and do what you needed to do today on such little sleep."

"You're saying you were worried about me."

"I guess. Eb, it's just breakfast. You don't have to eat it if you don't want. I promise you won't hurt my feelings."

"I'm just trying to wrap my mind around you, Joy."

"Your mind? I don't think I understand what you're saying,"

I respond quietly. It was just one night of sex—really amazing, great sex—but still, it was just sex. Did I step over some invisible barrier that Eb has? I'm not really experienced in relationships based just on sex.

Crap, I guess what we are doing can't be called a relationship.

"Last night you came into my room to rescue me?"

"You could have been murdered. I didn't know. You really should make sure you always lock your door."

"Wait. You thought there was a murderer in my room and all you had to defend yourself was a... *tin of cookies?*"

"I..." I stop talking, because that is kind of crazy, but there wasn't a lot to choose from on his desk.

"What did you think you were going to do? Send him into a sugar coma with the cookies?"

"Of course not. I was going to throw the tin at him or something. I don't know. I was scared. I don't exactly think clearly when I'm scared."

"If you were scared then why in the world did you come inside the house?"

"You could have been dying!"

"So you were rescuing me, you fucked me so good my balls are sore this morning, and now you're fixing me breakfast, even though you are late for work. Do I have all that right, Joy?"

"I fucked you?" I ask, my eyes widen with shock.

"Until my balls were sore."

"I don't know how to respond."

"That's okay, I don't want you to talk anymore," he says, grabbing my hand.

"You don't?"

"No," he says pushing his plate back on the table and then practically manhandling me by lifting me up on the table.

"Eb! What are you doing?"

He blows out a harsh breath through his lips and pushes his shirt that I'm wearing up to my hips. His shirt is so long on me that it falls low on my thighs. When cool air hits the inside of my thighs, I stop moving or arguing. He's not looking at me, but I am him and I see it.

Desire. Need. *Hunger.*

His fingers hook into the straps of my panties on my hips and he pulls. I lift my ass slightly to help get them off of me.

"Fuck. Your little cunt looks even better this morning."

"What are you going to do?" I ask Eb, but I know. I know and I'm wet just thinking about it.

"I'm going to eat my breakfast. Spread your legs for me Joy. Spread them wide for me baby."

"Yes…" I hiss the word, drawing it out because as I pull my legs apart, he lifts them over his shoulder. A moment later his tongue slides against the lips of my pussy, his mouth latches down against my clit and he groans as he sucks it and teases it with his tongue. His fingers bite into my ass and he pulls me even tighter into his mouth.

I fall back, close my eyes and let him eat his fill, all while praying he never does.

15

Eb

It's time I admit it. I'm in deep shit with Joy. There's no other way to say it. I like her. *I really like her.* Hell, I've been spending every night with her for two weeks and I'm not bored. I'm not looking at other women and I find myself looking forward for the time when she comes home. That alone is disturbing. For the first time in my life, I'm thinking about my place being home... with a woman.

She's a witch and has put a spell on me. I'd say she put one on my dick, but I like being with her even when I'm not fucking her.

When she called earlier to say she wouldn't make it by for dinner that she was finishing a rush Christmas order for the hospital alone, because Tina was sick, I wasn't happy. I should have used the evening to write, and fucking relax. I tried. The house we empty, it was too damn quiet and I missed Joy.

I missed her.

Christmas Joy is a witch and I'm in deep shit.

Instead of panicking however, I'm bringing Joy dinner. Like a... boyfriend. I don't remember ever being that in my fucking life.

"I'm sorry we're closed," Joy says, not even bothering to look over her shoulder when I walk through the front doors of the bakery.

Several things hit me at once. First, Joy's ass looks delicious in those tight black things she calls leggings. They cling to every damn curve of her body. The only thing I don't like is that red, Christmas sweater she's wearing that covers her ass. Still, she's bent over so at least the cheeks of her ass are visible and it's a spectacular view. Joy's ass is definitely cock-salute worthy.

Bending her over that counter, pulling those tight ass leggings down and fucking her ass-worthy.

I'd enjoy the view further but, I'm too mad.

"If you're fucking closed, then why isn't your door locked?"

"Eb?" Joy cries, turning around to look at me and there's happiness all over her face. She's glad to see me. She wants me to be here and that's just two more things that hit me. Things I like and definitely things that should add to my worry. Joy or I either one shouldn't be this needy to see each other, considering she just left my bad this morning after I fucked her senseless.

Hell. Joy might be more trouble than I imagined.

Before I can yell at her more, which would be nice because I don't like that she's causing so many thoughts and emotions to cloud my judgment, she cries and throws herself into my arms.

I mean that literally. Her body slams into mine. I remain standing, but it takes effort not to stumble back. I am forced to lock my arms around her too. Not because I want to hold her close or hug her. Purely because if I don't we're likely to fall.

At least that's what I tell myself.

Then, because I'm stupid and even though I shouldn't. Even though I should be running for the nearest airport to take me away from Juniper and all things Christmas Joy, I kiss her.

Our lips touch and I swear... it's like I haven't ever kissed her before in my life. Even now, after weeks of fucking her, it's like the first time my lips have been on her, it's like the first time my mouth has touched her lips, and the first time I've tasted her, explored her, drank from her.

Christmas Joy is a witch.

"How in the fuck do you always taste like vanilla?" I groan against her mouth when we break apart.

"I missed you," she whispers softly, hugging me closer for a minute. She squeezes me to her and that, combined with her words, seeps down inside of me and settle in a way I'm afraid of. Because, I'm starting to think I will never be able to let Joy go.

I step away from her, to catch my breath and hopefully breathe without the scent of vanilla clouding my head.

"If you're working late and here alone, Joy, you lock the god-damned door," I growl.

"Oh stop. Oh my gosh! What is that smell?"

I ignore her question, wrapping my hand against the side of her neck and hold her head so that she doesn't move. I tilt her head to look up at me, and bring mine down in close to her.

"You lock the door when you are alone at night, Joy."

"Oh come on, Eb. This is Juniper we are talking about. Here everyone knows everyone. I'm completely safe."

"You didn't know me until recently. Anyone could come into town. Bad people. People who could ruin that pretty smile of yours, or people who could hurt this body, that I love, in ways you might never recover from."

"The only person in Juniper interested in my body is you, Eb. Now stop joking around. What do you have in that bag? Is that Clarissa's chicken fried steak I smell?"

"I'm not joking with you. I want your promise that you will start locking the damn door when you're here alone after hours."

"Eb, you're being silly."

"Joy," I growl again. I'm close to turning her over my knee and spanking her ass for not being more aware. I know Juniper is a quiet town, but fuck, she has to know what this world is like. All you have to do anymore is turn on the news and see the shit

49

that goes down on a daily basis. Her not locking the door and being aware is not excusable. I don't want to think about Joy and this damn innocence she manages to keep—despite all the dirty shit we do in bed, being destroyed.

"Oh alright!" she sighs, pulling away from me and locking the door.

"Promise me," I urge her, needing the words, needing her to agree.

"If it's that important to you, I promise Eb. I'll make sure the door is locked when we close from now on. Better?"

"Only if you're telling the truth."

"I hereby solemnly swear to lock the doors when I'm here alone after hours," she says with a smile, and one hand over her heart like she was reciting the damn Pledge of Allegiance.

"Joy!"

"I swear! Geez. You're awful grumpy tonight Eb. I will lock the doors. Scout's honor!"

"Were you ever a scout?"

"Didn't we have this conversation once before?" she winks. "Do I get to see what's in that bag that smells so delicious?"

"I think I have a new goal with you, Joy," I respond, watching her closely.

"What's that?" she asks reaching for the bag. I pull it behind my back and the strangest thing happens. I find myself smiling in the middle of the bakery with Joy wrapping her body around me so she can reach behind me, Christmas decorated cakes everywhere, a giant Christmas tree in the corner with twinkling lights, and annoying Christmas music blaring over the shop's speakers.

Smiling and drowning in Christmas.

Joy is definitely trouble.

16

Joy

He brought me dinner.

It's crazy how the simplest things cause your heart to feel warm and full. I haven't examined what I'm doing with Eb, but for him to bring me dinner that has to signify something. *Right?*

Maybe he cares for me a little too. Maybe it's not just sex. That thought shouldn't make me so happy, but it does.

"Oh my God! I was right! It is Clarissa's chicken fried steak! God, I love this stuff. I didn't realize that was the special today!"

"It's not. And did you hear what I said?" Eb asks.

"No, what?" I ask, still taking the takeout containers of the bag and placing them on the counter. If heaven has a smell, I'm pretty sure it would be Clarissa's chicken fried steak.

Before I can open my food however, Eb pulls me close, making sure he has my attention.

"Why am I suddenly jealous of diner take out?" Eb asks, his deep voice rumbling.

"Because you're crazy?" I laugh. I place my hands on his shoulders to steady myself when he lifts me up off the floor.

"I need to start spanking you when you ignore me."

"I wasn't ignoring you," I laugh.

"You were and for a damn piece of meat."

"Well, I'm hungry."

"Kiss me and tell me you're sorry," he whispers, his lips so close to mine that I can feel his breath.

"What happens if I don't?" I ask, already leaning in so our lips almost touch, craving his kiss like I've never wanted anything else before.

"Maybe I'll take away your steak," he says, and I swear his lips brush against me and they're smiling.

"But I'm hungry," I say before we touch lips gently. He does that several times, bringing our lips together for the briefest of touches, but never giving a true kiss.

"Don't worry, sweetheart. I'll substitute the meat for a different kind."

"What kind is that?" I giggle, knowing exactly what he's talking about and suddenly I'm hungrier for him than for dinner.

"Joy!"

Before I can take Eb up on his offer, I can hear Margaret calling from outside. I sigh sadly, because I definitely wanted to play with Eb instead.

"Let's ignore her, maybe she will go away," Eb says, obviously feeling just like I do.

"These are her three hundred cupcakes. I don't think she's going to go away empty handed," I answer, resigned.

"Damn it."

"I completely agree," I tell him, giving out another heartfelt sigh. Sometimes I have the worst luck.

17

Eb

I load the last of the cupcakes into the back of the van, while Joy talks to the woman that I really don't like right now, Margaret something-another. I like to call her Margaret with the horrible timing.

"I don't know how to thank you Joy. I realize changing our order was last minute. The hospital just thought cupcakes this year was a better Idea than one big cake."

"It was no problem. Honestly I loved making the cupcakes and I agree. I think the cupcakes will make a big splash."

"I think it will too. I know the children will love it."

"Which is really all that matters, since this entire fundraiser is for them."

"Fundraiser?" I ask, because I'm getting tired of being ignored. I come up behind Joy and wrap my arms around her, pulling her into me. She resists at first and then relaxes against me. I rest my chin on the top of her head and wait for Margaret to answer.

"We're having a Christmas party to raise money for the children's cancer center at the hospital. We wanted to do something to try and make things a little better and use the money raised to help the parents."

"How does it help the parents?"

"The hospital funds programs to help parents with travel, free hotel rooms and paying for medications. Anything we can do. Sometimes it's not a lot, but in these cases every little bit helps."

"It sounds like a really good thing you guys do. I'd like to contribute. I could send in a donation."

"Joy can get you that information. She donates a tenth of all of her sales to the children."

"You do?" I ask Joy, looking down at her.

"It's nothing," she answers, refusing to look at me while her skin blushes with heat and discomfort.

"It's a lot. Especially with the sales you make this time of year," Margaret argues and I could only imagine because in the short time that I've known Joy, her bakery stays busy. I give her a squeeze, but I let it drop.

Margaret starts talking about the plans for the event, which apparently begins around lunch tomorrow. She stops abruptly when her phone rings. I'm hoping she decides to leave, but I've never been the lucky kind.

"I have to take this. Excuse me a minute, will you?"

"Of course," Joy says. As Margaret turns away to answer her phone. I pull Joy around to face me.

"How much longer do you think she'll stick around?"

"Eb! She'll hear you!"

"Good, maybe she'll leave so I can take you in the back and eat the dinner I have for you."

"I do want that steak," she says so sorrowfully I almost want to carry her in there and feed it to her.

"I wasn't talking about that. I was thinking more along the lines of stuffing my dick down your—"

"Oh no! What do you mean he pulled out? The party is tomorrow!" Margaret yells into her phone.

Joy tenses in my arms and turns to watch Margaret on the phone. Margaret argues with someone for a few minutes longer, before hanging up.

"What's wrong?" Joy asks, clearly concerned and because she is, I remain quiet, biding my time until I get Joy alone.

"Bruce is sick. He canceled for tomorrow."

"That's too bad," I interrupt, and caring less. "Joy we better go back in and start cleaning up," I announce, trying to hurry this along. Turns out I don't have it in me to be patient when it comes to getting Joy alone.

"Oh no! Do you have someone on standby?"

"Not really. There are other males at the hospital of course, but I'm not sure any of them will agree to stand in at such short notice. I'll have to make some calls tonight, which sucks because I have so much more decorating and things to oversee. As it is, I'll be lucky to get in bed before three in the morning," Margaret complains.

"There has to be something we can do. We'll just have to find another man."

"Another man?" I almost growl. I don't know what in the hell they are talking about, but it doesn't matter. I don't like the idea of Joy looking for another man for any reason.

"We'll have to, I'm just not sure we can find one on such short notice," Margaret answers. "We can't just use anyone close to the hospital. The children are too smart."

"I know some men who might be willing to help me. Let me make some calls and see if I can sweet talk one of them into doing it," Joy answers.

Maybe if I knew what in the hell they were talking about, I would be more cautious. Unfortunately, I'm not being cautious at all. I'm seeing red at the idea of Joy calling any man and sweet-talking them. In response, I do something completely out of character. I jump in head first without thought.

"I can do it."

"I can ask Brad and… *Eb?*"

"I can do it," I respond again, even though inside I'm begging for someone to shut me the fuck up.

"You can do it?"

"I don't see why not."

"Eb really, I can ask Brad or even Sam."

"I said I'd do it, Joy. Do you have a problem with me doing it?" I ask, annoyed and irritated that I'm fighting to do something just because I don't want her asking another man.

"No. I just didn't think you'd be interested."

"Well, you thought wrong," I grumble, starting to wish I'd just kept my mouth shut. Still, I kept her from asking *Brad* for a favor and she can save all her sweet-talking for me. I'm even starting to feel like I've won a victory here. Maybe if she talks sweet enough I'll let her make it up to me. I'll let her bend over while I shove my cock deep into her ass.

"This is amazing!" Margaret cries. "*The* E. B. Mason is going to be the Santa at our Christmas party!"

"Santa?"

"You just agreed to be Santa for the kids at the hospital party. Didn't you hear what we said? Will there be a problem?" Margaret says and I feel like I've had all the air stolen from my lungs and even if it means saving my life, I can't draw more in.

"Of course he knew," Joy says defending me. "Eb loves Christmas! That's how we met! He wanted help making his yard perfect," Joy adds, having no idea just how much she's terrifying me right now.

"That's great! He's just about the same size as Bruce! This will work perfectly! I can't wait to see you both tomorrow. Thank you two for all your help! I just know this is going to be the best Christmas party ever!"

"It will be! It will be the greatest!" Joy agrees.

"Yeah, the greatest," I whisper, needing a drink.

18

Joy

"Eb! We're going to get caught!" I tell him, but I'm laughing. I'm probably going to hell, but I'm pretty sure it will be worth it.

"Not if you're quiet. Now lean over the desk so Santa can show you why all the girls like to be put on the naughty list," he growls.

I do as he asks but I look over my shoulder at him, shaking my head no.

"That's really kind of creepy," I whisper.

Eb looks up at him and I have to resist the urge to giggle. He doesn't have the fake beard on yet, but he does have the white eyebrows. He doesn't have a shirt on, but the red velvet pants are there.

He smacks my ass and I gasp, but bite my lip to keep from calling out. I don't think it would be great for everyone at the party to discover Santa with his pants down. Besides that, I doubt Margaret would appreciate the way we're using her desk at the moment.

My body shakes as he spanks me again and again. Heat pours through my body like liquid steel. And now I don't have to keep from crying out, instead I moan.

"You're a bad, bad girl, Joy."

"I am?" I gasp, when his fingers move between my legs, brushing against my very wet pussy.

"Walking around in this tight little red dress all day, teasing Santa."

"I'm sorry," I whisper my head going down so that my forehead rests against the desk.

"I don't think you're sorry, Joy," his voice rumbles behind me like thunder and I can feel each vibration in my body and it all centers in my clit, causing my knees to go weak. I'm thankful the desk is holding me up when he delivers another smack across my ass. "I think you enjoyed it. Walking around, not wearing panties and teasing Santa. I bet you've been wet all night haven't you?"

I whimper. I have been, because I knew this was coming. I knew eventually Eb would find me and he would fuck me. I knew it, because he's right. I have been teasing him.

Every chance I've had today I've taunted him. I've leaned over in front of him. My dress is low cut and I've taunted him with my cleavage. I've bent over, making sure my ass was in front of him and it wasn't really an accident when a drop of icing fell between my breasts when I shared that cupcake with him.

"Answer me!" he growls. I look behind me to see he's undone his pants now. His hand is wrapped around his large cock, stroking it. There's a stream of cum sliding from the head and I thrust my ass out as I watch it drop against me. My ass is red from the spankings, red and heated. I can feel the cum slide against my skin and I want more.

I want a lot more.

"I have. I've been teasing you. I've been a very bad girl, Santa. It wasn't my fault, though."

"It wasn't?"

"No. I've been horny, Santa. I needed you to fuck me," I moan, only admitting the truth. Eb got me all hot and bothered this morning in bed, but refused to finish me off. He said it was my punishment for making him dress up as Santa. I've been aching for him ever since.

"I've been this wet. I've been so wet all night," I tell him, my body practically causing the desk to shake with me when he finally thrust his fingers deep inside of me, raking them against my throbbing clit.

"You need Santa to fuck you, Joy?"

"Yes, please, Santa. I promise if you do, I'll be good."

Eb pinches my clit hard, pulling on it and I cry out loudly, unable to stop myself.

I feel him wrapping my hair around his other hand, while he keeps manipulating my clit with his other. I can feel my excitement build and I know I'm going to come just like this. The inside of my thighs are painted with my need. I can't hold back much longer. I grab hold of the desk, trying to pull myself up on my weak legs, when he tightens his hold on my hair.

His hand moves from between my legs and I cry out again, but this time in disappointment. His hand moves to my face and caps over my mouth to help silence me and I'm grateful. I bite into it, because I want to yell at him to bring the hand back to my pussy. Eb lets go of my hair and I'm almost terrified he's going to leave me hanging again. I can taste myself on his hand, I'm so damn close. If he doesn't put me out of my misery, I might start screaming and throwing things. I don't care who finds us. Before I can try to move his hand and try and tell him that, his cock thrusts deep inside of me. My scream is a mixture of need and relief, but thankfully it's muddled against his hand. His other hand bites into my hip and he takes over my body, moving me how he wants me as he tunnels his hard, massive cock in and out of me.

"You better play with your clit, Joy, because Santa's coming hard," Eb groans. He didn't need to tell me that though. My fingers are already working my clit as I feel the first jet of cum stream inside of me.

"Yes," I hiss, even though he probably can't hear me.

"So fucking good, Joy. Your pussy is so fucking good. Everything I knew it would be and more. That's it!" he cries. "Squeeze my damn cock, milk all of that cum," he growls and I do it. I take everything I can from him.

Eventually he removes his hand, but he keeps me pinned on the desk by his warm body.

"Eb," I sigh, not sure what I want to say, just knowing I feel so much in this moment, I need to let him know.

"Fuck, Joy. You may kill me."

I whimper, because I feel the same about him.

"You don't clean up. Don't even think about it," he orders me. He sits in a chair, his pants still down, and pulls me into his lap, my dress still gathered at my hips. If I had the energy, I'd giggle. I'm going to have to clean this desk before we leave. Margaret would die if she knew.

"Eb, I have to. I have cum running down my legs."

"You have my cum, and I want it there. Every time I look at you tonight, I want to know you're so full of my cum that it's sliding out of you and you're clenching that tight little pussy trying to keep it inside."

"But…"

"Do it and Santa will show you what happens to girls who are on the nice list after the party."

"I doubt it could top the naughty list," I laugh, just now starting to get feeling back in my legs.

"Just wait and see, sweetheart," he grins, and I can't resist reaching up to hiss him briefly on the lips.

"We better hurry. They need Santa out there to read to the kids."

"Jesus. It's a good thing you just made me come," he grumbles, helping me stand.

I frown for a minute. Eb's been kind of grumpy all night about this party and dressing up as Santa. I've shaken it off, because I thought he was just whining over having to play

Santa, but more and more I think it's everything, the entire party. Which doesn't make sense. He promised me he loved the idea of going to the party with me. He loves Christmas, he's told me that over and over, and though I suspect, his love and mine aren't exactly matching, he at least likes it a lot.

Maybe he just woke up on the wrong side of the bed this morning, I rationalize, shaking it off. I heard him mention he's behind on a deadline and this probably isn't helping. I'll have to make sure to reward him later. I smile up at him, as I help him put on Santa's coat and after a minute he smiles back, squeezing my hand.

"Let's get this over with," he says and again I frown, but I nod my head in agreement. I don't know why I'm worrying, it's probably because being with Eb is so wonderful, I'm scared something will ruin it. Which is just silly. The last few weeks have been wonderful.

This will be the best Christmas ever and all because of Eb.

19

Eb

The last little boy climbs up on my lap and it's physically painful to see him. He looks so pale and weak. He can't be over six years old. It's fucked up that this is his reality, while other boys his age are running and playing ball and crying because they want the latest video game.

"What can Santa bring you this year?" I ask him, doing my best to keep my voice jovial, loud and booming. I suck being Santa, but it seems to be making Joy happy.

"Can you bring something to make my mommy happy?" the little boy asks and damn it, that is painful to hear. I can feel the pain lodge in my heart. I didn't sign up for this. It's bad enough Joy is having me prance all around as a jolly old fat guy, but I was happy in my little section of the world, I had my blinders on to everything and everyone else, they didn't factor into my day to day and I'm just starting to see how fucking screwed up the world truly is. *Or how I was.*

"Wouldn't you like something for yourself?" I ask the little boy, trying to shake off all of the emotions that are assaulting me.

"Mommy doesn't smile anymore. She's always worried about me. Can you bring her something to make her happy?"

I clear my throat, but I manage to get through talking to the small boy and reassure him. As the nurse helps him down from my lap I feel wiped. When I agreed to this damn party, I didn't know what I was agreeing to. I wasn't prepared for the sadness that is filling me right now. As I watch the nurses gather the kids and take them back to their rooms and the sad looks on the parent's face, I want to yell. How naïve are Margaret and Joy? How can this party help anyone? Margaret comes up and hands me a glass of punch.

"I thought Santa might be thirsty," Margaret says. I take it, pushing the fake beard down now that the kids are gone. I look around to find Joy and spot her in the corner of the room talking to some of the parents. I can hear her laughter from here.

"There's no way this party can help these kids, Margaret," I growl, still feeling raw.

"What? Of course it does. Did you not see the smiles on their faces today? It takes a lot to get these children to smile, Eb and you did that today."

"Not all of them," I grumble, the last boy's face still fresh in my mind.

"Unfortunately no. You're right, but you made a lot of them smile and that's a small victory and the money will help to make the parents lives a little easier. That's all we can do."

"More needs to be done," I grumble.

"Juniper is a small suburb. Our hospital has limited funds as it is. Most of these kids need advanced care, Eb. But, the sad fact is, a lot of the parents can't afford to travel to the bigger facilities as often as would be necessary. We do the best to fill the gaps," she says a little sadly.

"Money. It all boils down to money," I sigh.

"It always does. But, you should take comfort in the fact that because of your time tonight, quite a few kids here had one of the best nights they've ever had," she says like that's a big thing. I frown as she walks away. There's little solace in that, there has to be something more.

Before I can think on it more, I see my agent, Loretta, walk in the room and she's not happy. She's not happy any time actually, but right now the anger she normally carries around like other women carries purses, radiates from her.

Fuck. She must have gotten my email yesterday and drove straight here. I head to her in resignation.

This day just keeps getting better and better.

20

Eb

"Loretta what are you doing here?" I ask, trying to keep my tone civil. Really, she's a great agent, but I don't appreciate being hunted down. I sent her an email telling her that I had some issues and I wouldn't be able to get the manuscript in by the deadline and to ask for an extension. It's unusual for me, I'll give her that, but still writers do it every single day. It doesn't require a visit to be raked across hot coals. Which, from the look in her eye, is exactly what she has planned.

"Get out of my way fat guy, I'm on a mission," she grumbles and that's just like her going a million miles a minute, full steam, and failing to recognize what's right in front of her. Even if she didn't recognize my voice, she should at the very least recognize my face now that I've had the beard pulled down.

"Loretta, it's me," I explain, reaching up and snatching the hat and wig from my head.

She stops. Her shrewd eyes appraise me and I barely resist the urge to shuffle my feet underneath the attention. Loretta would have made a good interrogator during times of war.

"E. B.? What the fuck are you doing?" she growls, and calling me by my pen name. She refuses to use my real one. It's never really bothered me, but for some reason her sharp voice and the way she uses it now… *does.*

"What are you doing? I told you in my email I'd be in touch in a few days."

"And that's why I'm here. What the fuck are you doing dressed as a pervert. Is this shit why you are late on your manuscript."

"It's a Santa Claus suit," I growl.

"Same fucking thing. Who got it in their head one day and said: *Gee, I'm going to dress up in a red velvet suit and look like some little girl's grandpa and then ask her to sit and wiggle around in my lap and ask her what she wants me to give her for Christmas?*"

"Loretta," I caution her, my voice full of warning.

"A fucking pedophile. That's who. What the hell are you doing here anyway? You hate this Christmas bullshit as much as I do, E.B. That's always been one of the beautiful things about this relationship."

That's when I look around the room in a panic. I don't see Joy anywhere and hopefully that means she hasn't heard Loretta, which is a miracle since she is being loud and annoying. I grab her hand and literally pull her with me. She jerks her hand away, but she follows.

"Margaret, I need to use your office to meet with my agent," I tell Margaret as we pass. She agrees, her face troubled, which means she probably heard Loretta. I notice she looks at Loretta with dislike and that would fit. Loretta has a tendency to make *"friends"* everywhere she goes.

I get Loretta inside, turn on the light and close the door.

"Now, what in the hell are you doing here?"

Loretta walks to the desk and sits down, crossing her legs and taking off the black leather gloves she's wearing. She pulls a cigarette out of a small purse she is packing and after taking a puff of it, looks at me.

I hate the smell of cigarettes and I don't bother to keep the distaste off my face. Loretta doesn't care and makes that pretty clear when she flips me off. She really should have been born a man. She's a bigger dick than most men I've met, she definitely has bigger balls.

"How long have we known one another E.B.?"

I shrug. "A while."

"Ten years. Ten fucking years and in that time, especially since I've became your agent, how many times have you been late on a manuscript."

I shrug again.

"Not once. Not one damn time!"

"Then, I was due."

"Bullshit. You weren't even late the month you had to fly to Alaska to bury your dad. I think you wrote the entire time."

"My dad was an asshole."

"My point made. You hate people. You hate the world. You sit behind the typewriter and—"

"We use these new machines these days. They're called computers. You should try them Loretta."

"Fuck off. So who's the skirt?"

"What are you talking about?" I ask her stalling. I don't want her to know about Joy. Joy is mine. I'm not ready to share her yet.

"What piece of tail have you got your nose so far up that you aren't working."

"You're being stupid," I growl.

"Bullshit, again. I've been in this business for a long time. Enough to know men usually only fuck up their careers for one of two things. Dicks or Pussy. I would have figured you for one that likes pussy. But if you swing to the other side of the field, whatever. Who is it?"

"Shit. I don't do dick, Loretta. You know that."

"Then who is the skirt?" she asks and I walked into that pretty easily.

Fuck.

21

Joy

"Thank you so much for all your help, Joy. You went above and beyond," Margaret says and I wave off her thanks.

"It was my pleasure. Actually, next year I'd like to cater the event."

"That's such a wonderful offer, but I have to warn you our budget is pretty tight. We only play the current caterer half his fee. He waives the rest of it"

"No that's fine. I wasn't going to charge. I was going to do it for free."

"I can't let you do that. It's much too expensive."

"You're not letting me, I want to. Besides I can always write it off on my taxes," I joke. I look around the room and it's mostly empty now and the hospital staff that joined us, are all going back to work. "Have you seen Eb?" I ask Margaret when I don't see him anywhere.

"His agent showed up while you were in the restroom. He asked if he could use my office to meet with her."

"Oh. I hope everything is okay. He's been having trouble concentrating on his current project."

"I'm sure it's fine, although now that you mentioned it, she didn't seem like a happy camper."

"I might go see if they're done. I'd like to get home pretty soon. The judging committee will be out this evening to look at the decorations."

"I can't believe it's almost Christmas!"

"Me either, seems like every year it just keeps sneaking up on me," I laugh. "Thanks again for letting me help Margaret. I'll see you tomorrow."

"Bye Joy. You're an angel," Margaret calls back as I walk toward her office.

I didn't mention it to Joy, but I know Eb is behind and being here today probably didn't help matters. I'm praying he isn't in trouble with his agent, if he is then it's more than likely my fault. I'm actually hoping she's still around and I can apologize and play peacemaker between the two. Eb has many redeeming qualities but tact is not one of them.

I start to go inside and introduce myself, but as I gently push the door open I stop when I hear his agent.

"What piece of tail have you got your nose so far up that you aren't working."

Wow.

That doesn't sound professional at all. I flush with embarrassment, but I also instantly feel guilty too, because I'm getting Eb in trouble. I should have insisted he worked more and instead I asked him to be Santa today.

"You're being stupid," Eb growls, but I can hear the defensiveness in his voice. My hand tightens on the doorknob.

I miss part of the conversation, because I'm feeling horrible. Does Eb regret the time we've been spending with each other? It has been a lot, maybe too much. Maybe I should stop staying over at his house, at least through the week.

"It's not what you think," Eb growls.

"So there is a woman?"

"It's nothing serious. I'm just scratching an itch," Eb says and until this moment I never realized how much words could hurt. His simple words feel like a knife wound straight through my heart.

"I'd almost believe that if you were the old E.B."

"What do you mean the old E.B.?"

"The one I've been working with all these years. The one who can't stand Christmas, who can't stand parties and wouldn't be caught dead dressed like you are right now."

"I was helping out at the hospital."

"And the E.B. I know and mildly tolerate would never do that. He hates people. He'd rather have his fingernails ripped out one at a time rather than socialize."

"Damn it, Loretta."

"So I'm asking one more time. I think I deserve to know—since you're fucking up your career and ruining a hefty twenty percent that I get paid—who is the skirt?"

I can see through the door as Eb rubs the back of his neck. He's facing her, so I can't see his face. I don't really need to. I've heard enough. I start to back away, but I really don't do it soon enough.

"I'm still the same. I did all this to get in my neighbor's pants."

"Has your game slipped so much that you have to dress up like a freak in red pajamas to get your dick played with?"

"She likes Christmas. It gave me an in with her. I wasn't thinking past that, figured it didn't matter, because I'd be done with her by the time Christmas rolled around."

That wasn't just a knife wound.

That was a fatal blow.

It hurts so deeply that my breath burns in my chest. My skin instantly breaks out in a cold sweat and I stagger under the weight of the pain. I can't even stop a moan of pain from coming to my lips.

That's the one thing I wish I could take back, because the sound causes Eb to turn and face me.

"Joy," he says, his voice soft. He takes a step toward me and I take a step back. "Joy, honey," he says and the endearment just twists the knife in my heart. It also wakes me up. I spin around and run away. I hear Eb calling my name, but that just makes me run harder. I don't want to talk to him. I don't want to see him.

I never want to see him again.

22

Eb

"Fuck!"

"Let me guess. Comfort still isn't taking your calls."

"Her name is Joy and no she's not. Not that, that is any of your business. Why are you still here, Loretta?"

"Morbid curiosity mostly. That and you still haven't given me your completed manuscript."

"The manuscript can go to hell. I've got other things on my mind."

"I can see that. When's the last time you showered?"

"Why in the hell won't she take my calls? We're both fucking adults. Is it so much to ask that she talk about this sensibly?" I growl out, slamming my fist on my desk. That hurts like hell, but I welcome the pain. It gives me something to focus on besides the fact that it's been over a week now since I've spoken to Joy.

I've tried everything.

She's not been in her bakery. Her assistant Tina would barely speak to me too, but she said enough to let me know Joy is out of town.

Of course I knew that, because I've tried to find her at her house too. She's not been home. She never came home after the party, not even to pack clothes.

"I'm not good at matters of the heart, but I'm going to venture to say if I ever gave a damn about a man and I heard him say he was only using me to fuck me, I'd never want to see him again too."

I don't respond verbally to Loretta, though I do make a noise that I hope tells her to shut the fuck up.

Apparently it doesn't.

"But, I'd never have that problem because I'm sane. The opposite sex only has one use in my life. It's a philosophy I thought we shared."

"We did until Joy. If she had just stayed around," I mutter, staring at the phone and wishing she would call me.

"To hear you say worse things? I think she should be glad she left when she did."

"That's just it! It wasn't worse. I was trying to explain that even though that's how it started...*it's different now.*"

"Different?"

"Yeah. Joy's different. Shit there were nights we didn't do anything other than sleep."

"You don't sleep."

"I did with Joy," I grumble and I did. "When she was next to me, I was finally able to sleep. I wanted to sleep. I wanted nothing more than to close my eyes with her warm body wrapped around me and listen to her breathe. I wanted to make her laugh and listen to that sound for... *Shit. A lot longer than I got the chance.* Christ. She needs to know that she wasn't just a body to use until I grew bored. Not anymore and if I'm truly honest with myself she wasn't to begin with. Joy was different from the beginning. Joy was... *is... everything.*"

"Shit," Loretta says and I look up at her. Her face is full of shock. "Do you love her?"

Her words sound foreign to me, but I let them settle inside of me and they feel right.

They feel really right.

"Yeah. I think I do."

"Holy fuck-balls. You're in love with a Christmas freak," Loretta says, still in disbelief.

I don't bother to respond to that. Joy isn't a freak. She loved Christmas, but with her I was beginning to appreciate the season to.

I walk over to my window overlooking the lawn that Joy had painstakingly decorated. The lights twinkle against the fresh falling snow and it makes my heart hurt. It's beautiful. It's the kind of scene Joy would love.

It's the kind of scene she belongs in. She was made to sparkle in these lights with the snow coming down. As pretty as it is, it pales to how truly good and beautiful she is.

"She's an angel… a Christmas angel and I broke her," I whisper to my window, forgetting Loretta is anywhere around.

"Shit E.B. find your fucking balls. You want her, quit whining like some drunk poet singing prose and go get her," Loretta responds.

"I don't know where she is!" I growl, the hopelessness of the situation almost overwhelming.

"You said yourself you didn't spend all your time fucking her. Surely she gave you a hint or a clue to where she would be this time of year, or where she would stay."

"Nothing. She was planning on being home—*with me!*"

"Wha, wha, wha. Think with your head and not the one on your dick. Surely, you have an idea of where this chick would go to nurse a wound. What did she like? Maybe she tried to go find something that makes her happy."

"I don't know. I'm not a woman!" I grumble, scratching the stubble on my face. I haven't shaved since Joy left me. I've barely eaten. Mostly I've buried myself in a whiskey bottle.

"Well don't look at me, I'd go find another man with a bigger dick who made me forget you."

I let out an animalistic noise at the thought to Joy with any other man. Loretta holds up her hand and actually has the gall to laugh.

"Don't worry. I told you I'm not a normal woman. Start thinking of things she liked. Where would she go? Hell, it's Christmas, she runs a bakery and caters. Maybe she has a party tonight."

"No…" I whisper, but I turn around to look at the lights. But it's Christmas Eve… right?"

"Yeah? You may have gone off the deep end, but I have to tell you there's no pervert going to crawl down your chimney with Joy wrapped in a bow."

"Shut up, Loretta. I know where Joy is going to be," I say and for the first time in a week I feel hopeful. I look over at the grandfather clock in my office. "I know where she's going to be in an hour."

I practically run from the room. I need a shower and I have to clean up. By God, Joy will listen to me tonight and if she doesn't I'll tie her up and drag her back here until she does listen.

"Where are you going?"

"I have to get ready!"

"Ready for what?"

"To bring my woman home!" I tell Loretta over my shoulder, and I'm smiling.

Tonight Joy will be back in my bed… *where she belongs.*

23

Joy

"I don't know why you drug me here," I mumble as I sit in the cold metal chair at City Hall.

"Because it's Christmas and it's the light ceremony and trophy presentation. You're always here and just because Eb turned into a major asshole, you aren't going to let him steal this away from you," Tina answers, and I might understand what she's saying, but I think it's much too late.

I just want Christmas to be over. The lights and the snow mock me. The music hurts me. Right now I hate everything about Christmas. I hate it almost as much as I hate Eb Mason.

I should be thankful that at least he's not here. For some reason, I thought he might be. But, he's not and that's just proof I never meant anything to him. As if I needed proof. His words are haunting me as it is.

I was such a fool.

"I'd like to thank everyone for coming out tonight. It looks like we're getting a white Christmas! As hard as it's coming down, we will try not to keep you a long time. It'd be a shamed to get us all stranded at City Hall on Christmas."

I half-listen as the mayor drones on. I know Tina thought she was doing me a favor, dragging me here. But, she was wrong. I should have gone back to Tina's house and stayed there until this damn holiday was over.

I sit there for a few more minutes, but everything is a blur. I'm feeling sick to my stomach and it's so hot in here I can barely breathe. I just want out of here so I can catch my breath.

"I need to go outside for a minute," I tell Tina.

"But they're about to announce the trophy winner!" she argues.

"You can tell me who won. If I don't get out of here and get some air I'm going to pass out," I respond.

I'm lying, but I really just need to get out of here. Tina means well, but she just doesn't understand. Once I get this holiday behind me, I'll go home and erase all decorations and all signs that I was ever stupid enough to fall for Eb Mason.

"This year we're doing things a little different. We're going to award a prize to the best decorated home. There will be a first and second prize and the winners will get a fifty-dollar and a one-hundred-dollar gift card, respectively, from Grayson Hardware, compliments of Victor Grayson," the mayor announces and I frown.

Isn't that great?

The one year they give out a prize worth having and I haven't been paying attention to my home to even try to win. This is just another thing that is Eb's fault.

"In second place is the lady the whole town has come to rely on for her Christmas spirit and her delicious holiday goodies. Heck the town has even nicknamed her, Christmas Joy. Joy come on up.

I don't move. I feel like a deer trapped in the sites of a hunter's scope. I don't want to go up there and stand by the mayor. I don't want to stand in front of all of these people.

I just wanted to leave!

"Come on up, Joy," the mayor urges again and I look at him and then look at the door. I would have made a run for it, but Tina all but pushes me around her. I stumble into the aisle as people start clapping, leaving me no choice than to reluctantly walk to where the mayor is standing.

I'm going to kill Tina.

24

Eb

I watch from the corner of the room as Joy accepts her gift certificate. She looks so good. I have to clench my hands in fists to keep from going up and grabbing her. She will be mine soon enough.

"Our first place winner is a new resident to Juniper, but from the looks of his lawn he is definitely a welcomed addition. We're delighted to have award winning novelist E.B. Mason as part of our community and are pleased to announce he wins first place in this year's contest."

I watch as surprise comes over Joy's face. It shouldn't. She did all the decorating. She had to know she would win. She put her heart into decorating my house. Just like she put her heart into loving me.

I walk toward her and I see the exact moment she spots me. Her body jerks and I can see the tremble that shudders through her. She's going to run. I can see it in her eyes and I can't let her. I pick up my pace, my legs eating up the distance between us. She turns away just as I get there and my hand clamps on her shoulder. She physically coils away from me as if my touch is painful. I tighten my hand up on her forearm to the point it's probably painful, but I don't let her get away.

"Thank you, mayor." I answer, taking my gift card from him. I have no idea what Grayson Hardware is, but maybe I'll give it to Joy. From the look in her eyes she wants to kill me and there's probably something there to help her in that endeavor.

"You're welcome. Now, how about we—"

"If you don't mind Mayor, I'd like to address the citizens of Juniper for a moment if I could."

"Why sure, son. Go right ahead," he says standing back.

"I'll just go," Joy murmur's trying to pull away.

"No. I need you to hear this too Joy. Especially you."

"I don't want to hear anything you have to say."

Her words are more than understandable. I ignore them. I have one shot at this and if it doesn't work I'm not sure what I will do. Probably kidnap her and tie her to my bed until she does listen, because losing her is not an option.

"When I first came to Juniper I was a different man. I hated everything about the world I lived in. My agent said I was a caveman, a recluse and she was right. I lived for days I didn't have to have human contact. That's what I wanted."

"Because you're an asshole," Joy mutters and I smile.

"I was an asshole."

"You still are."

"Probably, but being in Juniper has changed me, Joy. Being with you changed me."

"It made you a bigger ass."

"I hated everything about Christmas before I came to Juniper and then this beautiful blonde with sparkling eyes offered to decorate my yard and I took one look at her and…"

"Decided you wanted to get your—"

"Sweetheart, there are kids in the audience," I warn her and I want to laugh. Joy is standing there looking up at me and she looks like she wants to kill me, but she's here and she feels something for me, even if it's hate. After a week of being without her, I'll take it. I'll take anything she wants to give me.

"I want to leave."

"One look at you, Joy and I changed."

"I. Want. To. Leave."

"You made me a better man, Joy."

"I made you get off," she hisses, and the audience gasps. Joy blushes like crazy and tries to pull away so she can leave.

I drop down to one knee, pulling out a ring box. I open it up and I can see when she realizes what is going on.

"Joy, I was a fool. I love you. This last week without you has been hell. I'm so sorry I ever hurt you, but if you had stuck around you would have heard me tell Loretta that you are nothing like I expected. You're more than I ever dreamed. You're everything to me Joy and if you give me the chance I'll prove it to you."

"Eb..."

"Will you marry me, Joy?"

"But, we don't know each other and you said..."

"I was a fool. And I don't care how long we've known each other, I just know I love you and without you I will slowly die inside. Marry me, Joy."

25

Joy

"But… you said you were just…."

I stop. I'm so lost. I can't talk. I don't know what to say. I just keep staring at the ring resting in the jeweler's box. The diamond sparkles against the black velvet and then blurs as tears begin to fall from my eyes. My heart slaps against my chest, beating erratically.

"You didn't hear it all. I was an idiot, Joy. I was, but I'm not now. This last week without you has been miserable. Please, sweetheart, forgive me, marry me. Shit, Joy put me out of my misery."

"Eb, I don't think this is a good idea."

"Fair enough, but if you don't take me back and I have to warn you I'm going to carry you out of here and chain you to my bed until I make you agree."

My mouth drops open at his threat. My eyes widen when I see the look on his face, because I'm positive he's not joking. Suddenly that fear inside of me let's go. As crazy as all this is, I want it.

I want Eb.

"Then I say no," I answer, keeping my face as blank as I can, wiping the tears from my eyes.

"Joy, please. Sweetheart, you have to listen to me."

"But, I'm definitely open to you taking me back home and convincing me to say yes," I add, interrupting him before he can say anything more.

"I was just shooting my mouth— Wait... What did you say?"

"Take me home, Eb. We have a lot to celebrate."

"That sounds like a yes to me," he answers.

"It's not a no, but I probably need more convincing," I hedge, but he understands because he's already sliding the ring on my finger.

"I love you Joy," he whispers, bringing my hand up and kissing my finger and the ring.

"I love you, Eb."

"Enough to marry me tomorrow?"

"On Christmas? You hate Christmas."

"It's growing on me and if you marry me, it will be just one more reason to love it."

"Then, yes. Definitely yes, Eb." I whisper, as he takes me in his arms. I hold him close, looking over his shoulders where my hands are on his back, pulling him to me as tight as I can. The ring is staring back at me as bright as the Christmas star and it fills me with warmth.

This is the best Christmas ever and Eb is the sole reason why.

Epilogue

JOY

Two Years Later

I LOOK around the children's wing which has been transformed into a winter wonderland, that would rival the North Pole. I cater this Christmas party every year, but this one is extra special. My gaze drifts over to the green velvet chair that looks like a throne. Sitting in it is my husband, Eb, dressed as Santa.

We've been married for two years today.

They've been years filled with a little bit of arguing, because Eb can be stubborn, but they've mostly been filled with laughter and love.

Definitely love.

My heart squeezes inside my chest as I see the gentle way he's holding our son Nicholas in his arms as he reads *T'was the Night Before Christmas*, to him and to the other children which are gathered around him. Tears sting my eyes as I watch our one-year old son reach up and play with Santa's beard.

Nicholas is really too young to understand Christmas or who

Santa is, but he does recognize his father's voice and our little boy could listen to his daddy read for hours on end. Mostly because that's something Eb does with Nicholas every night. A ritual that Eb started while I was carrying our son and has kept doing every night since.

Nicholas is our Christmas miracle. I had so much trouble carrying him, the doctors weren't sure he was going to make it because he was born four months premature. Nicholas proved them wrong and just grew stronger and stronger every day. Eb likes to say he inherited his mother's determination. I know the truth, however. Nicholas is stubborn, just like his father.

Eb looks over at me and even through the fake white beard, I know he's smiling. He smiles all the time, but he never smiles more than at Christmas.

He says this is his favorite time of year now, because every year I do something to make his life better at Christmas. Last year it was the birth of our son.

I wonder what he will think of this year's Christmas surprise?

My hand goes to my stomach and I rub it gently. My wedding ring catches the light and sparkles and I can't help but smile.

I'm pregnant.

The doctors told me the chances were slim that would ever happen, because I had to take fertility medication just to conceive Nicholas.

I smile, because I know something the doctors don't know.

Christmas is a time for miracles and that's just what our child is.

A Christmas miracle, just like that night two years ago when I took a chance and married the love of my life after a whirlwind courtship. Or, just like my son defying all odds and coming into this world, growing healthy and strong last year.

Which fits really, because this is the most wonderful time of the year—especially since Eb Mason walked into my life.

I walk over to my family and listen as my husband says the last few lines of the story and I know in that moment, I have everything I could ever want.

"Merry Christmas to all and to all a good night," Eb says, closing the book and I lean down to hug him and Nicolas. Eb kisses my cheek. "Merry Christmas, sweetheart," he whispers, where only I can hear him.

"Merry Christmas Santa," I whisper back. "Merry Christmas."

Afterword

Thank you for taking the time to read Eb and Joy's story. This might be the first book released, but hopefully it won't be the last. I'm already working on another story about a hot Alaskan alpha who orders a wife through an online site, and gets a lot more than he bargained for.

If you enjoyed this story, I'd like to encourage you to leave a review. It's very hard for authors—especially new ones—to get seen without your help. If you'd like to stay up to date on my new releases, below are links. You can also sign up for my newsletter and be the first to know when I release or giveaway goodies.

Thank you again!

Tory

Newsletter: http://bit.ly/2BQIRkH

Facebook: https://www.facebook.com/Tory-Baker-575083209283480/

Email: torybakerbooks@gmail.com

29101254R00059

Printed in Poland
by Amazon Fulfillment
Poland Sp. z o.o., Wrocław